Princess Poppy
Pop Star
Princess

written by Janey Louise Jones
Illustrated by Samantha Chaffey

YOUNG CORGI

POP STAR PRINCESS
A YOUNG CORGI BOOK 978 0 552 55703 0

Published in Great Britain by Young Corgi,
an imprint of Random House Children's Books
A Random House Group Company

This edition published 2008

3 5 7 9 10 8 6 4 2

Text copyright © Janey Louise Jones, 2008
Illustrations copyright © Random House Children's Books, 2008
Illustrations by Samantha Chaffey

FSC
Mixed Sources
Product group from well-managed
forests and other controlled sources
Cert no. SGS-COC-1940
www.fsc.org
© 1996 Forest Stewardship Council

Young Corgi Books are published by Random House Children's Books,
61–63 Uxbridge Road, London W5 5SA

www.princesspoppy.com
www.rbooks.co.uk

Addresses for companies within The Random House Group Limited can be
found at: www.randomhouse.co.uk/offices.htm

THE RANDOM HOUSE GROUP Limited Reg. No. 954009

A CIP catalogue record for this book is available from the British Library.

Printed and bound in Germany

Princess Poppy
Pop Star Princess

Check out Princess Poppy's website
to find out all about the other
books in the series

www.princesspoppy.com

With love to Lucy Guthrie,
a true princess

Honeypot Hill
To the City
Saffron Thimble's Sewing shop
The Orchards
Paddle Steamer Quay
Healing House & Garden
The Worthington's House
Lavender Valley Garden Centre
Aunt
Melody Maker's Music shop
Lavender Lake
Bumble Bee's Teashop
Lavender Lake School of Dance
Hedgerows Hotel (where Mimosa lives)
SCHOOL
Peppermint Pond
Rosehip School
Summer Meadow
Christmas Corner
Wildspice Woods

Honeysuckle Cottage
(Poppy's House)

Poppy Field

Forget-Me-Not Cottage
Grandpa's House + office

...t Cottage
...ranny

Blossom
Bakehouse

Cornsilk Castle
and
Courtyard

...golds
...al
...re

Village Hall

Sages Vet Surgery

...st Office

Beehive
Beauty Salon

Riverside
Stables

Barley Farm
The Meadowsweet's
House

River Swan

Honeypot Hill
Railway Station

To Camomile Cove
via Periwinkle Lane

N
W E
S

You're a Star...

competition
coming soon in
Camomile Cove ✦ ✦ ✦

Chapter One

Poppy and Honey were so excited. Along
with Poppy's older cousin, Daisy, and her two
friends, Lily and Rose, they were the Beach
Babes. In just two weeks' time they were
going to be taking part in the local heats
of the *You're a Star!* talent contest, which
were being filmed in Camomile Cove.

Poppy and Honey had been backing
singers for Daisy's band ever since the
Smuggler's Cove High School Battle of
the Bands the summer before and they

couldn't wait to perform with them again.

"It will be so cool if we win," said Poppy breathlessly. "I can't wait."

"But won't there be loads of other really good bands taking part?" asked Honey, already feeling a bit nervous about the whole thing. "Do you think we have a *real* chance of winning?"

"I think we will definitely be the best," replied Poppy confidently. "Saffron is going to make our stage outfits, Madame

Angelwing's assistant, Claudine, is going to teach us a brilliant dance routine, and I know that Daisy, Lily and Rose are working on a really cool new song."

"Ooooh, how exciting!" replied Honey. "I love dancing!"

"Me too," giggled Poppy, "and it's mainly you and me doing the dancing because the others will be playing their instruments. I bet none of the other bands will have a proper dance routine. I've made a plan with Daisy that we'll meet her, Lily and Rose at the Lavender Lake School of Dance on Saturday at ten o'clock. They're going to play us the song and Claudine is going to start teaching us our dance."

"What's the new song like?" asked Honey.

"Ummm, I don't actually know yet because they're still writing it," explained Poppy. "Daisy said that they're meeting in her summer house every day after school to work on the words and the music."

"I wish I had a cool cousin like you do," sighed Honey, who thought her life might be rather dull without the connections of her beloved best friend.

"Daisy practically *is* your cousin, Honey!" laughed Poppy. "You see her just as much as I do."

On Saturday morning, Poppy and Honey set off to meet Daisy and her friends. They were desperate to hear the new song and so excited to be involved.

When they arrived at the dance studio, Daisy, Lily and Rose were already there. Poppy hugged her cousin and said 'Hi' to the other two girls,

and Honey shyly followed suit.

"Is the song finished?" asked Poppy. "Can we hear it?"

"Hang on a minute," laughed Daisy. "We've only just got here. We need to set everything up first."

"OK," replied Poppy, "but can you at least tell me what the song's called?"

"It's called *Chocolate Sundae Girls*. It was inspired by our favourite treats at the Lighthouse Café! And, even better," Daisy continued, "the owners of the café, Fleur and Harvey, have said that if we win the competition, we'll all get free chocolate sundaes for the rest of the year!"

Poppy thought that the Lighthouse Café was the coolest place on earth and she knew that their chocolate sundaes were heavenly. "Wow!" she said. "Deeelicious!"

Just then Claudine came out of the staff room, ready to get to work, and Daisy pressed PLAY on the CD player. The Beach Babes' new song filled the room and all the girls, including Claudine, couldn't help dancing and humming along to its catchy pop tune and brilliant words:

Sittin' at the window table
Waitin' for our dreams to come,
We don't have designer labels,
We are nobodies to some.

Give our order to the girl,
She brings a treat for us to share,
Chocolate sauce for us to swirl,
Fluffy ice cream everywhere.

(chorus)

And ooh, we are the Sundae Girls,
A secret club, as cool as ice,
The Chocolate Sundae Girls.
Oh yeah!
(repeat)

Livin' life- a social whirl
Cool as ice, but twice as nice,
OK, so we want to thrill,
But we are sugar more than spice.

So, when will the dreams come true?
Our ships come in, our luck begin?
You'll never see us gettin' blue,
'Cos we can take life on the chin,

(chorus)

'Cos, oooh, we are the Sundae Girls,
A secret club, as cool as ice,
The Chocolate Sundae Girls!
Oh yeah!!

Daisy, Lily and Rose were thrilled that everybody liked their song – they'd put so much hard work into it. But there was still lots to do before the talent contest.

"Let's get going with the dance routine for Poppy and Honey!" urged Daisy. "Claudine, what do you think we should do?"

"I have this idea that we should base it around street café life. What do you think?" she asked as she showed the girls a scenario she had in mind, where the younger girls

started singing while sitting at chairs at a round table in the middle of the stage. Gradually they would get up and start dancing and singing around the table, picking up their tambourines and shaking them from time to time.

The Beach Babes all thought it was really good idea, and so original. Poppy and Honey just couldn't believe they were part of it. The dance part gave them much more to do than before. Poppy felt like the luckiest girl in the world.

Chapter Two

After their rehearsal Grandpa came to meet his two granddaughters, Poppy and Daisy, and the other girls. He was particularly keen to meet up with Daisy as he didn't see as much of her as he would have liked. She was always so busy with her part-time job, school, her friends, her pony and her other hobbies.

"I expect you're hungry after all that dancing," smiled Grandpa as he walked into the dance studio. "How about I treat you all to lunch at Bumble Bee's Teashop? It may not be quite as cool as the Lighthouse Café, but the food is second to none."

"Yes please," chorused Daisy, Poppy and Honey.

"Thanks, Mr Mellow," said Rose politely.

"Lunch sounds great and so does Bumble Bee's. Daisy has told us all about it," added Lily.

Honey felt very proud that her granny's teashop had such a good reputation with Daisy's cool friends.

All the way to the teashop the girls chatted about the contest.

"We've really got to practise playing the music now that the words are in place," said Rose, who was very musical.

Everyone agreed that there was still masses of hard work ahead but they were all sure it would be worth it in the end, especially if they won their heats and went through to the finals in the City.

Poppy dropped back to talk to Grandpa. "I really, really hope we win. It would be so exciting. Daisy, Lily and Rose have written such a cool song."

"Well, I'm looking forward to it too," agreed Grandpa. "But remember—"

"It's the taking part that counts!" interrupted Poppy. "I *know* that, but I still want to win, Grandpa!"

Grandpa smiled. "There's nothing wrong with a competitive spirit, darling, as long as you can control it – and are still pleased for your rivals if *they* win."

Poppy gave Grandpa's hand a squeeze and skipped off to catch up with the others. They had reached Bumble Bee's Teashop and Poppy was dying to tell the older girls exactly what they should order.

"Hey, girls, I know the menu really, really well, so if you need any help choosing, just ask. My favourite is the baked potato with cream cheese and bacon filling. Oh, but I also love the cheddar cheese and tuna melt. But then again, the fish and chips are the best ever! And the home-made apple cream cakes are yummy . . . and as for the toffee doughnuts. Deeelicious! And you really must try the fresh fruit smoothies – they are so yummy!" she advised.

Daisy and her friends laughed.

"You haven't really helped us to decide, Poppy. It *all* sounds great," said Lily. "I wish I could have a bit of everything."

As they settled down at a table and decided
what to eat, Granny Bumble greeted them
warmly and began taking their huge lunch
order. Grandpa sat at a nearby table and took
out his newspaper, tuning out the noisy
chatter from the girls' table. It was great
having granddaughters, but sometimes it was
nice to get away from it all!

"Joseph Mellow! How are you, old
fellow?" said a voice from the other side of
Grandpa's newspaper.

He put it down, recognizing the familiar
tones. "Philip Forster! What a lovely
surprise!" he said, greeting his oldest friend –
and rival – Colonel Forster, with a warm
handshake.

"Take a pew, old boy. I'm just treating this
pop group over here to lunch – they're going
to be in some contest over in Camomile
Cove," Grandpa explained, looking at the
girls, who were practising the chorus of the

new song as they waited for their lunch to
arrive.

"Ah! The talent contest. My granddaughter Lilac's in that too," replied the
Colonel. "Remember, my daughter Martha
is married to Hugh Farrington, the
headmaster of Smuggler's Cove High
School? She's a lovely girl, their daughter,
Lilac. What a talent," he continued as he sat
down. "She's just like my Martha. Y'know,
Martha should've been on the stage. Very

16

nearly was a star, was our Martha!"

"Is that right, Philip?" asked Grandpa, rolling his eyes. Everything in the Colonel's world was always bigger, better and more successful than anyone else's.

"In fact," continued Colonel Forster, "I've rented a cottage over in Camomile Cove to be near the family during the contest – and to take a trip down memory lane. Remember the year I discovered the wreck of an old pirate ship in the cave at Sandy Bottom? What a lot of work I did on that!"

"*You* found it, you say? *I* saw it first and showed it to you, Philip Forster!" replied Grandpa. "And I cut the timber to repair it, remember?"

The two elderly men bickered affectionately about who had been responsible for discovering the ship and restoring it. They were still as competitive as they had been when they were schoolboys, and the Colonel's talk of taking a cottage in Camomile Cove had set Grandpa thinking . . .

After lunch, once all the girls were safely back home, Grandpa settled down in his sitting room to make some telephone calls.

"Silly old fool," he chuckled to himself. "You've got to beat the Colonel to that old pirate ship, haven't you?"

The next day, which was Sunday, Grandpa, Granny Bumble and Honey came over for lunch at Poppy's house, just like they did every week. It was a Cotton family tradition and Poppy loved it. It was as if they were one big happy family, even though Granny Bumble and Honey were not actually related to her.

When Grandpa arrived for lunch, bringing his usual gift of some flowers from his garden and a box of chocolates, he looked very pleased with himself indeed.

"What's up with you, Dad?" asked Poppy's mum. "Why the big grin?"

"Well, I've got a surprise for everyone," replied Grandpa. "Sit down and I'll tell you all about it."

They looked at Grandpa as he began to speak – none of them had any idea what the surprise might be but they couldn't wait to find out!

"Now, you know the girls are competing in *You're a Star!* in a couple of weeks' time? Well, I thought it might be nice to stay in Camomile Cove since that's where the contest is, so I've rented a lovely new beach-front lodge there. It's called The Pebbles and it sleeps ten, so there's room for all of us. I went to see it late yesterday afternoon and it's wonderful. We have it for a week starting from next Sunday. I know it's all a bit last minute, but I hope you think it'll be fun."

"How exciting," said Poppy's mum. "It sounds amazing. Thank you, Dad!"

"Oh, I am glad you like the idea," smiled Grandpa. "Not only will the Beach Babes be able to rehearse as much as they like but we can all have a fine seaside holiday, which I think we're in need of." (He left out the bit about the house being fancier than Colonel Forster's rented cottage, and even nearer to where he thought the old pirate ship was!)

Poppy's parents were thrilled with Grandpa's surprise about the beach house. They couldn't afford to pay for a holiday this year without Grandpa's help: the twins were taking up Mum's time and she'd hardly made any new hats for ages, so their income was way down from normal.

Poppy's dad arranged to take a week off work, Granny Bumble employed Gertie Jenkins as a temporary manageress to take care of Bumble Bee's Teashop and the Blossom Bakery, and Mum started organizing everything they would need to take with them.

Everyone was really excited about the holiday, although it was the talent contest that was occupying Poppy and Honey's thoughts the most.

Chapter Three

Over the next few days, Honey and Poppy arranged for their pets to be looked after while they were away and laid out the clothes they were planning to take with

them. They practised the words to the new song as often as they possibly could, singing in the tree house, the playroom, Poppy's bedroom and

down at Riverside Stables too.
They knew exactly where to
come in with their backing
vocals, adding some depth
with their sweet, tuneful
voices. They had a couple

more dance
sessions with
Claudine and
there were
also two full
band rehearsals
in Daisy's
summer house at
Camomile Cove.

In the middle of the week, Daisy, Rose
and Lily came over to Honeypot Hill to visit
Saffron's Sewing Shop. Since Saffron was
going to be making their stage outfits, she
needed to take all the girls' measurements
and show them the fabrics she had in mind.

"I've already got a fabulous idea for your outfits – but it's going to be a surprise!" she explained. The girls couldn't wait to see what she came up with. "I'm also going to ask Holly Mallow to make some jewellery to go with your outfits and I'm sure Lily Ann Peach will come over and do your hair!" she continued.

"Wow! That sounds amazing. We're so lucky," said Poppy.

The days before the trip were spent packing picnic things, bathing suits, buckets and spades, toys and clothes, plus favourite foods. By early Sunday morning, the

Cottons, Grandpa, Honey and Granny Bumble were finally ready to make their way over to the neighbouring coastal town for their holiday.

To get everyone properly in the holiday mood, Grandpa had booked them all tickets on the paddle steamer. He thought that a gentle boat trip down the River Swan to the coast would be by far the most relaxing way to travel to Camomile Cove. So they all made their way up to the quay, where Mr Crowther helped them aboard the *Paddle Princess*.

Poppy was absolutely thrilled when she saw The Pebbles, the beachside lodge Grandpa had rented. It had just been built by Mr Atkins, the local builder from Strawberry Corner, and was painted a soft cream colour with lots of huge picture windows and balconies. To the back was a grassy garden with lots of space for tennis and rounders. To the front was a decking area for eating out, which led to a private jetty where a little fishing boat was moored. They even had their own stretch of pebbly beach, which is how the house got its name.

"This is amazing!" exclaimed Poppy, itching to see the inside.

"Nothing but the best for my family and friends," said Grandpa, smiling proudly.

The inside did not disappoint. It was all very clean and simple, with smooth tiled floors and vanilla walls adorned with splashy modern art paintings of sunny

coastal scenes. Squashy cornsilk-yellow sofas faced out onto the bay. The cheerful family-friendly kitchen with adjoining dining area all looked well furnished, with natural wood fittings and masses of everyday essentials. Grandpa had even ensured that there were two high chairs for the twins.

"Come and look at our bedroom, Poppy!" cried Honey, calling down from the third floor.

Poppy raced up the wooden staircase to reach her friend. "Wow! I love it!" she squealed, taking in the sweet attic bedroom, with windows overlooking the sea.

There were two beds with sunshine-yellow covers, a pretty wooden dressing table, a large painted wardrobe and a cheerful patterned rug.

"Isn't this the *best*? A beach holiday *and* a talent contest. It's *perfect*!" said Poppy. "Let's unpack quickly. Mum said that lunch would be ready soon. Then we can go to the beach and then, after that, Daisy wants us to head over for a proper rehearsal."

Mum and Granny Bumble produced a lovely simple picnic lunch on the table on the balcony. As they ate their lunch, they all enjoyed the breathtaking view of rocky outcrops, pale sandy beaches, aqua sea and sailing boats bobbing to and from the harbour.

By mid-afternoon, everyone was having a heavenly time down on the main beach, which was reached along a path near The Pebbles. Angel and Archie were both

bucket-and-spade mad, even though they mostly wore the buckets on their heads as hats rather than making sandcastles. Dad was more relaxed than he had been in months and he and Mum were laughing the whole time. Poppy and Honey were splashing about in the sea, and Grandpa and Granny Bumble were chatting away happily as they relaxed in two stripy deckchairs.

"Remember the Punch and Judy shows we used to watch on the beach, Joseph?"

recalled Granny Bumble. "Weren't they grand? And the colourful beach huts and ice-cream stalls. It was super. Those were the days!"

"They certainly were," agreed Grandpa. "It's great to be back."

"You used to hang out on the beach with Philip Forster every summer, didn't you?" asked Granny Bumble.

"Yes," mumbled Grandpa. "In fact, I believe he's spending the summer over here too."

"Oh, how nice – I didn't get a chance to chat to him the other day at the teashop. I was much too busy making lunch for the girls. We should have him over to supper one night," suggested Granny Bumble.

Granny Bumble, Grandpa and Philip Forster had all been in the same class at Smuggler's Cove High School many years before and had been great friends.

"Maybe we should," replied Grandpa.

"Maybe you should what?" asked the familiar voice of Colonel Forster as he walked up behind the two deckchairs and greeted his old friends.

Chapter Four

"Ah, Joseph. Taking up the lion's share of the beach, I see!" teased the Colonel. "What brings you over to the Cove?"

Grandpa cleared his throat. "We've taken a little house for the week," he said. "That's it behind us."

The Colonel almost choked on seeing the smart modern beach house. "Very good. Looks flashy," he commented. "Can't beat the little fisherman's cottages, though. They're so full of character."

"Any luck with finding the pirate ship?" Grandpa asked casually.

"Still looking for the cave, old boy!" said the Colonel. "Still looking!"

"You must come over for supper this week, Philip," said Granny Bumble. "It would be lovely to catch up."

"Well, thank you very much. That sounds splendid. I'll check my orders with Martha and let you know if I've got any free evenings. I'd best be off now," said the Colonel, "I've got a pirate ship to find!"

"Honestly," chuckled Granny Bumble, "I can't believe you two are still so competitive after all these years. You're behaving like a pair of overgrown schoolboys!"

Later that afternoon, Poppy and Honey strolled down to Daisy's house with Dad and the twins. Just as they passed the village shop, Poppy noticed a news-stand selling the local paper, the *Camomile Chronicle*.

The Camomile Chronicle

HEADMASTER'S DAUGHTER FAVOURITE TO WIN TALENT CONTEST

"Hey, look, Honey. Isn't it that girl Daisy knows? Lilac Farmer, or something?" said Poppy.

"You mean Lilac Farrington," replied Honey. "She's so pretty, isn't she?"

"Dad, can we buy a paper, please?" asked Poppy.

Dad agreed and the girls decided to tuck it into Poppy's bag and take it to read with the rest of the band.

"Hi, girls!" said Rose as Poppy and Honey walked into the summer house.

"Hi!" they replied as they both flopped onto a beanbag and joined in the general chat.

"How's the house you're staying in?" asked Daisy. "I can't wait to see it."

"Oh, it's amazing!" Poppy replied. "We're having such a cool time here."

"It's brilliant that you're staying in the Cove," said Lily. "We'll be able to fit so much more practice in before the contest."

"I'm worried that Lilac Farrington and her band are going to win," Daisy said.

"Lilac always wins everything and comes top in all the exams at school. Our song is really good, but they *look* so good. Plus, Lilac was telling me they have a great song too. They're doing all their rehearsals down in a cave near Sandy Bottom because they don't want to let anyone hear it before the sound check."

"Oh, that reminds me," said Poppy as she fished around in her bag for something. "Dad bought us a local paper.

There's something in it about the contest and Lilac. Look!"

Daisy grabbed the paper and quickly scanned through the article, reading certain bits aloud:

"'*I'm feeling lucky – I really think we could win this,*' said Lilac. '*And* You're a Star! *is my all-time favourite show!*' she continued . . ."

"How is it that she gets asked to give interviews in the newspaper and we never get the chance?" wondered Lily.

"That's because her dad, our beastly headmaster, Mr Farrington, is friends with one of the judges. They always ask one local person, apparently, and our local judge is Mr Simms, the bookseller, who provides the school with all their textbooks," explained Daisy.

"It's so not fair," complained Rose.

"I know," agreed Daisy. "But as long as we're original and we practise loads, I suppose we've got as good a chance of winning as Lilac has, even if our dads aren't friends with one of the judges and we're not being interviewed in the local paper."

She pulled out her file all about the

contest. "See – on this entry form it says: *Original material will be favoured*."

"Well, our song is *totally* original, because we wrote it ourselves," said Rose. "Let's forget about Lilac and concentrate on us. There's nothing we can do about it anyway."

"Who else is appearing in the contest?" asked Honey, trying to steer the conversation away from the gorgeous Lilac, who seemed to be denting everyone's confidence.

The older girls told them about a local Elvis impersonator called Jamie Johnston. And a sweet little girl called April, who was singing a medley from *Grease*.

"Hey, guess what my brother told me about the boys' band, Caves 'n' Rocks?" said Lily. "Apparently they've written a song all about cars called *Gearhead*."

"Wow, that sounds super dull – nothing to worry about there then," smiled Rose.

Although no one said it aloud, they were quite convinced it was only Lilac and the Mermaids that stood between the Beach Babes and the big finals in the City.

"Let's get on with our rehearsal, shall we?" said Daisy positively. "We've really got to work on the tricky musical bits to make sure we're note perfect on the big day. Your dad will be collecting you and Honey for supper soon, Poppy, so we haven't got much time today."

The next morning, the girls met at the Lighthouse Café. With all the fuss about the contest – some of the people from the local TV station were starting to arrive – it was even busier than it usually was during the summer holidays. As soon as they entered the packed café, they saw Lilac and her band sitting at one table and the members of the *You're a Star!* crew at another. Lilac smiled and waved at Daisy and her friends.

"Look, that's Johnny McDonald!" said
Lily, recognizing one of the judges. "How
cool that we're in the same café as him!"

They couldn't see a free table right away,
but the owner, Fleur, soon found them a
booth next to the one where Lilac and her
band were sitting. As soon as they had
settled in, Lilac leaned
over to say hello.

"Hi there,
Beach
Babes!
How's the
rehearsing
going?" she
asked, flicking her hair and looking over at
the judges' table.

"Pretty good, thanks. How about you?"
Daisy replied.

"Oh, amazingly well, actually. It's really
coming together," she said. "See you on

Wednesday at the sound checks.
Good luck!"

"Yeah, you too," said Daisy, hoping with
all her heart that the Beach Babes would
win the contest.

"At least we'll hear their song at the
sound checks and see what we're up
against," said Rose quietly so that Lilac
and the Mermaids couldn't hear.

"Let's just run through our stage
movements again. We can mark up my
song sheet," said Lily.

The girls jotted down all their moves on
Lily's sheet, and after enjoying a delicious
milkshake each, they decided to go their
own separate ways.

Poppy and Honey arrived back at The
Pebbles to find Mum and Dad packing a
picnic lunch to take down to the beach.
The twins were playing with building blocks
on the kitchen floor, Granny Bumble was

in the garden, flicking through her favourite
cookery magazine, and Grandpa was
poring over a map of the coast.

"What are you looking at that for?"
Poppy asked him.

"Well, I'm going off on a mission to find
the old pirate ship in one of the caves down
at Sandy Bottom," announced Grandpa,
"before that pesky Colonel Forster tracks it
down!"

"You sound very competitive, Dad,"
laughed Poppy's mum. "I thought you were
against all that sort of stuff?"

"I am. Well, most of the time I am anyway, except when it comes to old Forster. I remember when he beat me in the maths challenge and came first in the triathlon. Oooh! Now he even says he discovered the pirate ship and restored it. But I found it and I did all the work too!"

Everyone laughed. Grandpa was usually so cool and calm about everything. Poppy had certainly never seen his competitive streak before.

"Philip tells me he has a granddaughter in the talent contest too," said Grandpa, trying to steer the attention away from his rivalry with the Colonel. "I think he said she's called Lilac. Do you know her?"

Poppy and Honey's jaws both fell open.

"Lilac Farrington?" they chorused.

"Um, yes," replied Grandpa, "that's right. Her father is the headmaster."

"She's brilliant, Grandpa," they told him.

"I'm sure she is," Grandpa said, "but if she's anything like her grandfather, she won't always win by fair means."

Chapter Five

Grandpa made his way along the familiar yellow sands, remembering the wrecked pirate ship he had found all those years ago. Just as he reached the inlets where he had spent so much of his boyhood, he bumped into the Colonel and they decided to look for the ship together.

They spent several hours looking in many of the caves – without success.

"Hang on. This looks like it, Joseph!" exclaimed the Colonel suddenly as he recognized the opening to a large cave.

Grandpa followed him in through the entrance to the dark, damp cave. It did indeed look familiar and it was certainly large enough to fit a pirate ship in. As they went further, they thought they could make out the shape of their ship in the shadowy distance.

Soon they could hear voices – laughing and singing. They went in further to explore, their eyesight straining through the gloom. Sure enough, their pirate ship was nestling gently in shallow waters, but dancing all over it were Lilac and the Mermaids! They were singing a rather tuneless ditty about a mermaid lagoon.

"This is rubbish!" said one of the girls.
"We'll have to think of something better
than this before the sound-check rehearsals
on Wednesday night."

"I know," said another. "It's going to be
sooooooooooooooooo embarrassing – the
Saturday performance will be on local telly
and everything!"

"I think I might have an idea!" said Lilac.
"I've got something that might help us back
at my house. Let's go!"

As they were packing up their things,
Grandpa and Colonel Forster walked up
to the ship.

"Lilac, dear," said Colonel Forster, "what
are you doing here?"

"Oh, hi, Grumps!" said Lilac sweetly.
"We're just rehearsing for the contest. In
fact we're just heading back to my house.
See you later."

"Jolly good," replied Colonel Forster.

"I know you're going to do me proud, sweetheart."

When the girls had gone, Grandpa and the Colonel explored the ship just as if they were little boys, and argued good-naturedly over who had found it.

As Grandpa made his way back to the beach house, he found himself thinking about the talent contest. *Lilac and the Mermaids aren't nearly as good as Poppy seems to think they are*, he mused. *I don't think they're such a threat after all. I must tell the girls.*

Grandpa arrived back at The Pebbles to find that everyone was either playing on the beach or swimming, so he decided to settle down with his paper and enjoy some rare peace and quiet. It was a real treat being on holiday with his family, but they were awfully noisy!

The next day, after breakfast, Grandpa and Dad were left in charge of everything while Mum and Granny Bumble went food shopping. They were having a huge barbecue party that night for some friends and family from Honeypot Hill, as well as Daisy's parents, Delphi and Daniel, and her brother, Edward, and Lily and Rose's families.

Dad was in a bit of a pickle, trying to keep the twins amused, doing the dishes and playing a board game with Honey and Poppy all at once.

"What can I do?" asked Grandpa.

"Maybe you could entertain the twins while I get Poppy and Honey organized for their rehearsal at Daisy's," suggested Dad.

"Right-o – I'll get the building blocks," replied Grandpa.

"OK, girls," said Dad, sounding much more in control of things now that Grandpa was handling the twins. "Get ready for your rehearsal – you're due at Daisy's in fifteen minutes. Now, I must get on with the dishes."

Poppy and Honey ran to brush their teeth and change their T-shirts. With a brush of their hair and a smear of lip gloss, they were ready to go.

"Bye," they chorused as they skipped through the kitchen towards the back door.

"Have fun, girls," called Dad, "and don't forget, you need to be back here in good time for supper."

"Oh, just one thing before you go," said Grandpa, suddenly remembering what he'd seen in the cave the previous day. "Don't say I told you so, but you haven't got much to worry about with regard to Lilac and the Mermaids. I happened to hear them rehearsing yesterday and, well, they're not a patch on the Beach Babes!"

Poppy grinned. "I hope you're right, Grandpa. I can't wait to hear everyone else's songs at the sound check tomorrow!" she said.

Honey and Poppy walked quickly over to Daisy's, feeling full of excitement. The rest of the Babes were already tuning up their instruments.

"Hi, girls!" said Daisy cheerfully when she saw Poppy and Honey. "We're going to do a quick run-through of the full routine."

"Oh, by the way, Lily," said Rose, "did you find your song sheet at the Lighthouse Café?"

Lily shook her head. "Nope, 'fraid not. Fleur and I looked everywhere but we couldn't see it. I could have sworn I left it there. Oh well, never mind. I know the whole song by heart anyway, and we all know the dance routine too."

"You can share mine if you need to," said Rose.

"Are we all ready?" asked Daisy, keen to get on.

"Oh yeah!" chorused the girls.

After a really thorough rehearsal, the girls collapsed in a heap, exhausted by the concentration. They had to admit, it was as good as it could be. The song sounded great and the dance routine was ideal – even if they did say so themselves!

"See you tonight at our party!" called Poppy to Daisy and her friends as she and Honey left the summer house. "Remember to bring your instruments, and we'll see what all our friends think about *Chocolate Sundae Girls*."

"OK, Princess!" called Daisy. "See you later!"

The girls strolled home, chatting breathlessly about everything that was going on – and about what to wear that night for the party. It was all just so exciting!

Later, as Poppy and Honey got ready in their attic room, they heard familiar voices downstairs. So many friends had arrived from Honeypot Hill for the party: Saffron and David Sage, Sally Meadowsweet, Lily Ann Peach, Holly Mallow, Abigail, and Sweetpea and Mimosa and their families too. And they had all promised to come back to Camomile Cove on Saturday for the show.

Saffron came armed with a bag full of nearly finished dresses, as well as scarves, hair clips and sequinned mules for the girls to accessorize their stage outfits with. Holly had brought along some brand-new jewellery designs for them to choose from too. After a delicious spread of food – barbecued and roasted meats, herb-crusted fish, buttered and minted new potatoes, tender plum tomato salads and fruit puddings with honey-sweetened cream – they all settled down in the big sitting room to listen to the Beach Babes. This would be the final rehearsal before the sound checks the following evening. The girls set up the

huge balcony at the front of the house as a stage, tested their instruments, then began to sing *Chocolate Sundae Girls*.

The whole room fell silent. Everyone was very impressed by the wonderfully high standard of the girls' work. When they took their bows, there was a huge outcry of stamping, clapping, cheering and shouts of "Bravo!" The girls smiled proudly and hugged one another as the whole audience declared them unbeatable in the contest.

Chapter Six

After a quiet day on Wednesday, with walks
on the beach, antique shopping and street
café coffee stops, the Beach Babes – along
with their families, who were coming to
watch the performance and lend moral
support – headed down to the beach in
good time for the sound-check rehearsals.

The families took their seats while the
girls had a team chat behind the scenes. A
big stage had been set up with lots of sound
technology, fancy microphones and amps.

Poppy really hoped that everything was working properly. Then she reminded herself that the whole point of tonight was to see what problems there might be and to fix them in time for the big show on Saturday. Daisy would have to get used to the drum kit provided, and they would see how much space they had to move around in too, as they might need to adapt their dance routine slightly.

The judges were seated behind a big desk. Johnny McDonald was flanked by sweet-faced Julianna, a former pop star herself; on the other side was Bronwyn, a record producer, and next to her was GT, a successful band manager. The production crew and presenters wandered around taking instructions from producers and directors as well as engineers. Suddenly it hit Poppy what a big occasion this was. It was all so professional. Maybe their dream of being as

successful as their favourite girl band, Rubies and Pearls, would come true after all.

① The Turtles
② Wave
③ Blossom Darling
④ Shooting Stars
⑤ Abba Tribute Band.
⑥ The Surf Dudes
⑦ Kit Sullivan
⑧ Caves 'n' Rocks
⑨ The Beach Babes
⑩ Lilac & the Mermaids.

All the performers were given a sound-check order list and the Beach Babes saw that they were due to go on stage second to last, just before Lilac and the Mermaids. But as all the performers milled about backstage, Poppy noticed that Lilac's dad was in a huddle with the judges. It soon became clear that he was asking if his daughter's band could go on before the Beach Babes. Lilac was apparently too nervous to go last. When the judges asked the Beach Babes if they minded going last instead, they had a quick chat and decided that in fact it would be an advantage as everyone would go away remembering their act best, even though it was only the sound check and not the real contest.

"OK then," agreed Daisy, the unofficial spokesperson for the band, "that's fine with us."

Lilac smiled. "Thanks, girls, that's really sweet of you."

Poppy, Honey, Daisy, Rose and Lily all took their seats backstage, anxious to hear what the competition was like, but feeling quite secure about their own chances, especially after what Grandpa had said about Lilac and the Mermaids.

The first few acts were pleasant enough, and a little girl from Strawberry Corner called Blossom Darling was especially cute with a song she had written herself about ballet. Any screeching in the sound system was quickly adjusted by the production crew. But so far, it didn't look like any other group had put the same time and effort into their numbers as the Beach Babes had. They were sure all their practice was going to pay off. Poppy thought that Caves 'n' Rocks were really good, despite what Lily's brother had said about their song, and so were an Abba tribute group – although they were not original.

Soon it was time for Lilac and the Mermaids to perform. Lilac got up on stage, followed by her band, and took the microphone. She looked very glamorous in a mini-dress and high heels. The rest of the

Mermaids were dressed much more simply,
so that Lilac looked even more stunning.
Her long blonde hair had been newly styled
and, with a flick of her golden tresses, she
began to sing. Her song was: *Chocolate
Sundae Girls*.

The Beach Babes couldn't believe what
they were hearing. Surely Lilac didn't think
she could get away with pinching their song.

Granny Bumble, Mum, Dad, Uncle
Daniel, Aunt Delphi and all the other
parents were completely dumbstruck.
Grandpa was appalled. He had heard Lilac
and the Mermaids practising their song in
the cave two days before and it wasn't this
one. How had Lilac got hold of his girls'
song? He looked over at the Colonel, who
had also heard Lilac's dreadful rehearsal in
the cave, to see him smiling proudly, just like
Grandpa should have been at his two

granddaughters. But what was odd was that Mr Farrington, rather than looking happy for his daughter, looked rather disconcerted and puzzled.

Chapter Seven

Lilac did not sing brilliantly at all, but the fact that the song was good enabled her to pass it off quite well. Her friend Fern Zitelli was on guitar, with Lulu Lamont on drums, and they did a passable cover version of *Chocolate Sundae Girls* even though it was nothing like the Beach Babes' version and they had no backing vocals or dance routine to speak of.

The judges seemed very impressed. As far as they knew it wasn't a cover version of another song; it seemed truly original, as well as catchy.

Poppy felt hot tears pricking in her eyes. Daisy's palms were warm and clammy. Honey was in tears. Rose and Lily had never been so furious. How could this have happened to them?

Suddenly Lily began to sob. "It's all my fault! Remember when I dropped my song sheet in the Lighthouse Café and me and Fleur couldn't find it the next day? Well, Lilac was at the next table – she could have stolen the song sheet then. And when their own song didn't shape up, she must have decided to use ours instead and then ask to sing before us!"

"What a rotten thing to do!" exclaimed Daisy, but it was the only explanation that made any sense.

As Lilac's band took their bows on stage, Lily spread the word of what might have happened amongst their families. They were all appalled. They knew that the girls had been singing that number all along and had written it themselves.

Soon it was time for the Beach Babes to take the stage. But instead of the whole band going up, Daisy walked on alone, bravely took the microphone and tried to explain what had happened.

"We will not be able to take part in the

contest because our song has been sung by Lilac and the Mermaids. We're not sure how this happened, but a song sheet of *Chocolate Sundae Girls* went missing from the Lighthouse Café."

There was a gasp of confusion from the audience, other performers, the judges, presenters and crew. Then there was a hush. Johnny McDonald walked towards Daisy and took the microphone from her.

"Well, folks, looks like there's been a bit of confusion here. But, hey, that's what rehearsals are for! I guess that's it for tonight. Thank you, everybody. We need to try to get to the bottom of this."

As the Beach Babes were being comforted by their families, Lilac, Lulu and Fern walked past. None of them even looked at Poppy and her friends. They couldn't believe that after all their hard work and commitment they were out of the contest and it seemed like there was nothing they could do about it.

Daisy's mum, Delphi, couldn't stand it — it was so unfair. She jumped up onto the stage and spoke into the microphone, managing to say her piece before she was escorted off by a burly bouncer.

"You haven't heard the last of this. I don't know what Lilac and the Mermaids are up to, but they won't get away with it. I saw my daughter and her friends write that song and I will not rest until the truth comes out — and the truth *will* out, I am sure of it!"

There was nothing more anyone could do or say to make a difference so they returned to The Pebbles feeling very frustrated, angry and disappointed at the way things had turned out. Poppy had never felt so low. It seemed there was no way out of this horribly unfair situation.

Back at the house, they all settled down in the living room.

"Right!" said Poppy's dad. He hardly ever got angry, but now he was feeling furious. "Let's discuss what options are open to us here. This is a very difficult situation."

"Why don't we confront Lilac and her band and get them to confess?" suggested Mum. "She must have a heart. I've always thought she was very sweet. Sometimes I think her dad puts too much pressure on her to be the best at everything. Maybe she just needs a bit of sympathy."

"Hmmm, I think we should talk to people in the town and see whether they can shed any light on this," said Rose's dad.

Granny Bumble thought this was way too complicated. "Why not just wait? The truth will come out all by itself. I'm sure Lilac's father knows what's going on. He can't stay silent about this – he's a respected member of the community. I saw him last night when our girls were performing their song on the balcony. He was out for a stroll on the beach with his dog. He even stopped to listen and gave a wave."

Daisy's brother, Edward, nodded in agreement. "I saw him too!"

"Is that so?" asked Grandpa. "Well, I think my old friend the Colonel might know more about this than he's letting on too.

He was with me when I heard Lilac and the Mermaids singing their dire song in the cave. But he can't see any wrong in that girl."

"That's all very well," replied Lily's mum,

"but we don't have much time. I think we should see whether they can re-enter the competition with a different song."

There was a mixture of reactions to all these ideas, but most people thought the only quick way round the problem was for the girls to get started on a new song right away.

"In the morning I'll check that you're still allowed to perform with a new song, girls," promised Dad. "And you'll have to get your heads together and come up with one as soon as possible. I know you can do it, you're all so talented. And of course, if we can get the judges to see the truth before Saturday, then you can still sing *Chocolate Sundae Girls*."

Poppy had rarely seen her dad so bossy. He was *determined* to find a way through for his princess and her friends.

Chapter Eight

The next day was Thursday and the week
that had started so joyously was rapidly
going downhill.

After breakfast Dad and Grandpa went
over to the Farringtons' house to discuss
things with Lilac and her dad. They rang
the bell nervously. They were both desperate
to sort things out and protect the girls from
any more heartache.

After a couple of minutes a rather
embarrassed-looking Mr Farrington appeared.

"Hello," said Dad. "We're sorry to bother you so early, but we wondered whether we could have a chat with you and Lilac about what happened yesterday. I'm sure there's a perfectly reasonable explanation, but we'd like to get to the bottom of it and to hear Lilac's side of the story too."

Before Mr Farrington could say anything Lilac came to the door, smiling sweetly. "Hi, Mr Cotton and Mr Mellow, I thought you might come over," she said.

"Well, I suppose you'd better come in," said Mr Farrington as he ushered Dad and Grandpa into the sitting room.

"I wonder if we could see the song sheet you used for *Chocolate Sundae Girls*, please?" asked Grandpa.

"Of course," Lilac replied. "I'll just go and get it."

She came back brandishing a song sheet for *Chocolate Sundae Girls*. It had all been written out in her own perfect handwriting.

"That is clearly Lilac's," said Mr Farrington. "She's done nothing wrong, have you, darling?"

"No, Daddy," Lilac assured him. "The Beach Babes must just have got really nervous when they saw how good our song was and thought it was better to tell lies rather than lose face by not doing such a good performance as me and the Mermaids."

"Well, there you go. Now you've got to the bottom of it," said Mr Farrington. "Now, if you'll excuse us, we've got things to do."

Dad and Grandpa said goodbye and walked forlornly back to The Pebbles. They felt they had made things worse, not better, and decided not to say anything about their conversation to the family.

"Farrington knows the truth. He couldn't meet our eyes," said Grandpa.

"Yes, but Lilac's not ready to face the truth. I think she's lied so much, she has started to believe it really is her song now," concluded Dad.

Grandpa nodded. "All she cares about is winning. She doesn't care how she does it. Our girls have got commitment – that must count for something. Lilac will come unstuck at some point. Even if she wins with our girls' song, she'll never be able to think of another!"

Dad agreed. He knew that being on the side of truth was all that mattered, but the sense of injustice was stinging his heart nonetheless.

Back at The Pebbles, Granny Bumble was clearing up the breakfast. She had lovingly prepared a hot spread, with fluffy scrambled eggs, crispy bacon, buttery mushrooms and piles of buttered toast. But no one had been hungry, so it was all going to waste.

"It's our word against theirs," mumbled Mum as she wiped the twins' faces and took off their bibs.

"Listen to an old girl like me!" said Granny. "I keep saying it and no one will listen. This will sort itself out in a way you can't imagine. I am confident the truth will win through. The fact is, our girls haven't cheated, so we should feel proud of them, whatever happens. It's only a contest."

Poppy and Honey hoped more than anything in the world that Granny Bumble was right, but neither of them could see how it was going to happen.

Dad went out again almost immediately, this time with Poppy and Honey, and dropped by the temporary office of *You're a Star!*, which was in the *Camomile Chronicle* building. He asked if they could re-register with another song.

An administrator came through to speak to Dad and reluctantly agreed that the girls could be included if they came up with a song by Friday tea time.

"That gives us less than two days to think of a new tune, words, dance routine and everything!" wailed Poppy as Dad took her and Honey round to Daisy's summer house.

Daisy, Lily and Rose were already there, feeling very de-motivated and still shocked. On hearing the news about the new song being acceptable, they tried to jot down some notes but they were struggling for inspiration.

"Why don't we write about school?" suggested Lily. "How awful it is – especially with a headmaster like Farrington."

The girls perked up a bit at this idea.

"Yes," agreed Daisy. "We could call it *High School Blues*. That could work. But it won't be as cool as *Chocolate Sundae Girls*. That was the best song we've ever written."

All the girls murmured their agreement, but they did not want to be left out of the contest so they settled down to some serious song-writing.

"How does this sound?" asked Lily.

"That's a great start, Lil!" said Daisy. "We could really work with that. But I can't think of a good dance idea and there's not enough time to ask Claudine."

"Let's just concentrate on the song, shall we?" said Rose. "I don't feel in the mood for dancing anyway. Why do such unfair things happen? Why do the goodies always win in the movies, but in real life the baddies always win?"

"No, Rose," Lily said sagely. "It's just that in real life the goodies take much longer to win. But let's not give up. Let's get on with this song – I'm sure we can make it work."

Daisy burst into floods of

tears. "But the other song is great too — how dare she do this to us! It's so mean."

The girls comforted their friend, who was normally so positive. Somehow they would get through this — they knew they were in the right.

Chapter Nine

Back at The Pebbles, Grandpa had some
time to think and came up with another
idea. He turned to his two distraught
daughters, Lavender and Delphi, both
nursing cups of tea and aching over the
problems facing their beloved girls.

"What if you were to go down to the
cave where Lilac and the Mermaids rehearse
and keep their stuff? After all, that's where I
overheard their song. Perhaps that way we
could find some proof of what they've been

up to. Maybe our girls' lost song sheet will be there – who knows?"

Delphi and Lavender liked the idea and thought it was worth a try.

"Let's take the girls with us. They deserve to see what's going on in there," said Mum.

"OK, why not wait until they're finished in the summer house?" said Grandpa. "Maybe I'll come too, to save you getting lost."

So, after Daisy, Poppy and Honey had had some lunch, they all followed Grandpa down to the beach. As they passed the newsagent's, they saw yet another newspaper article with Lilac's face splashed below it. MY SONG IS A WINNER! screamed the headline.

Poppy and Daisy were furious.

"Ignore it!" said Mum. "We know the truth, and hopefully everyone else will know it soon too."

Before long they were creeping around sand dunes and through long, jaggy grasses, scrambling over rocky outcrops, heading down to the beach. Soon they reached the mouth of the big cave. They entered as quietly as possible – they could hear girls' voices and see shadowy figures in the gloom. They had stumbled on Lilac and the rest of the Mermaids having a full-scale row. Poppy and her family hid behind a cluster of rocks near the entrance to the cave and listened to what was going on.

"This is all about you, Lilac. You don't care about us!

You just want to be famous. You're using us," stormed Fern.

"You wouldn't even be in the contest if I hadn't found that song sheet!" retorted Lilac.

"So, you admit you found it then?" raged Lulu.

"They shouldn't have dropped it. Finders keepers, losers weepers," said Lilac, who was beginning to sound a bit wobbly.

"But it's their song!" said Fern. "I feel sick. We're cheats and it's all your fault. You told us you'd written that song!"

Lilac burst into tears. "It's too late to back down now," she sobbed.

Poppy and the others couldn't believe their ears.

Just then, Fern and Lulu stormed past them without even noticing that they were there.

"We're going to tell the judges the truth!" Fern called back to Lilac.

"No!" screamed Lilac. "I'll do anything. Please. Stand by me. I can't admit I lied. Can't we just withdraw from the contest and hope everyone forgets?"

"Stop it, Lilac!" yelled Fern. "Face the truth. I don't know how you thought you'd pull this off. We should have realized from the start that we needed to spend more time on our song and to practise loads – like the Beach Babes did. We want to win too, but not like this!"

Lilac was still sobbing and shrieking.

Delphi, Lavender, Poppy, Daisy, Honey and Grandpa stayed out of view until a hysterical Lilac had also left the cave. They emerged from their hiding spot and walked over to the lovely ship Grandpa had found all those years ago.

"No wonder Dad's proud of it and so cross that the Colonel pretended he had found it himself!" said Poppy's mum to her sister.

"What a family!" agreed Aunt Delphi as they began to look around for Lily's original song sheet.

"It's not here. It must be in her house," said Daisy.

"Don't worry, darling," said Aunt Delphi.

"I think her friends are going to help us get to the bottom of this situation. Let's go back."

Daisy looked at her younger cousin. "Truth will out!" she whispered.

Poppy grinned happily back at her.

When they got back from the cave, Poppy, Honey and Daisy called an urgent band meeting in the summer house. Daisy told the other girls what had happened in the cave and suggested that rather than preparing a whole new song and routine, they must just hope that Lulu and Fern would keep their word and that the truth would come out by Friday.

All the girls decided to go their separate ways for the evening, each desperately hoping that things would work out but trying really hard not to get their hopes up too much.

"Let's all meet in the Lighthouse Café in

the morning," suggested Rose. "After all, we have no need to hide ourselves away. We've done nothing wrong."

"Good idea," replied Daisy.

It was agreed they would gather at ten o'clock. They all had an early supper and went to bed. No one could believe how the mood had changed since the beginning of the week. That night, everyone at The Pebbles was still nervous that Fern and Lulu would chicken out of telling the judges about Lilac.

The next morning, all the girls and their mums met at the Lighthouse Café as arranged. They had still not heard any official good news about Lilac and the Mermaids. The café was brimming with people, but as soon as they arrived, Fleur excitedly invited them into the kitchen to tell them the news she had been hearing all morning.

"Lilac's band members have apparently kicked her out, saying she can't sing for toffee. Which she can't! And they're furious that she is hogging all the attention and leaving them out in the cold. The word is that they admit she found your song sheet here and took it!" concluded Fleur, grinning from ear to ear.

At first the Beach Babes were silent. Then they began to whoop with delight. Maybe things were going be all right after all.

"I knew the truth would out," Aunt Delphi said, smiling.

"Hang on a minute!" replied Mum. "Let's go down to the *You're a Star!* office to check all this before we get too excited, shall we?"

Chapter Ten

Mum and Aunt Delphi squeezed hands – there really was no way this could be just a rumour – Fern and Lulu must have revealed everything just as they'd threatened to the day before. Daisy, Poppy, Honey, Lily and Rose kept very quiet but were bursting with excitement inside – they so wanted it to be true.

The whole gang headed down to the *You're a Star!* office. When they got there, they saw an announcement posted on a board in the reception.

We now have proof that Lilac and the Mermaids did not sing their own song at the sound check and as a result the band has been disqualified from the contest. We regret any problems their behaviour has caused, particularly the actions of lead singer, Lilac Farrington.

Aunt Delphi read it out loud so all the girls could hear what it said. They didn't jump or yell or laugh. They just cried with relief and joy. They were going to be able to perform *Chocolate Sundae Girls* after all!

"Hey, I was just about to ring you," said Johnny McDonald as he strolled into reception. "Why don't you all come into my office for tea and cakes while I try to make it up to you girls?"

"Yes, please," they chorused, hardly able to contain their excitement about being back in the contest.

After juice and flapjacks with Johnny, Poppy and Honey were desperate to rush back to The Pebbles and tell everyone the wonderful news. They found Grandpa deep in conversation with Colonel Forster. It was clear that the Colonel knew what was going on and was in the process of explaining everything to Grandpa.

"Joseph, I can only apologize, old fellow," said the Colonel. "I don't know what came over Lilac. I can only think that we've put too much pressure on her, particularly her father, and she just couldn't bear the thought of disappointing us. The poor girl is very upset and very sorry for what she's done. She just always wants to win. I suppose she might have inherited her competitive streak from me. But you know how it is, Joseph – you love them whatever they do wrong. And I'm sure she'll learn from this and try to make it up to your girls and their friends."

Grandpa nodded, feeling very sorry for his old friend, and for Lilac too, and he was just a little bit ashamed of himself for still being so competitive. Friendship was all that mattered – life was not a competition. Grandpa wished his friend well and saw him out.

Poppy and Daisy hugged their grandpa. No one wanted to dwell on what had happened; they just wanted to get on with the show.

After a very thorough rehearsal on the stage at tea time, when the girls were allowed to try out the mikes and sound system as they hadn't had a chance on Wednesday, all the Beach Babes collapsed into an early bed.

The next day, just before lunch, Saffron, Holly Mallow and Lily Ann Peach arrived from Honeypot Hill.

"Look what we've brought!" exclaimed Saffron. She showed Poppy and Honey the five gorgeous dresses she had made. They all had simple bodices and flower petal skirts. For Poppy there was a bright red dress; for Honey, a yellow one. Saffron had made a pink one for Rose, a cream one for Lily and a pure white dress for Daisy.

"Wow! They are so pretty!" said Poppy.

Holly had brought gorgeous jewellery for them to choose from, while Lily Ann had picked fresh flowers to decorate their hair.

"Thank goodness it's all back on!" said Granny Bumble, seeing the trouble their friends had gone to. "My nerves can't take any more!"

By mid-afternoon, all the girls were dressed in their new flower dresses, and their hair looked stunning with their namesake flowers woven in place. They couldn't wait to get on stage and sing their song.

When they arrived at the beach venue with all their friends and family in tow, the Beach Babes were surprised to find Lilac Farrington waiting for them. Her face was very puffy and she looked like she had been crying. Her parents, both looking rather awkward and uncomfortable, gently nudged her towards Poppy and the others.

"I . . . I w-w-want t-t-to s-s-say sorry,"

she sniffed. "I'm really, truly, very sorry. I just wanted to win so much. Lulu and Fern didn't know anything about what I'd done. It was all me. I have learned my lesson and I'll never do anything like that again. Please don't hate me for ever," she sobbed.

Her mum, Martha, began to cry too.

Even though Poppy and her friends were still upset about what had happened and cross with Lilac for what she had done, they felt really sorry for her. Yes, she had caused them a lot of pain and suffering, but her parents had made her feel she always had to win or come top, so it wasn't really all her

fault. And it was very brave of her to say
sorry to them face to face.

"Lilac, it was a horrible and cruel thing to
do to us but we don't want you to worry
any more. We understand why you did it,
even if it was still really wrong. Why don't
you come and support us in the contest?"
suggested Daisy. "If you cheer us on,
everyone will see that you didn't mean us
any harm and that there are no hard
feelings."

Lilac nodded through her tears. "I'll sit in
the front row and scream as loud as I can
for you!"

Everyone smiled and the Beach Babes
went backstage to prepare, hugging all their
families and friends before they did so.

Poppy felt as though she was entering
another world as they went into a makeshift
dressing room. They were brought bottles of
water, which they desperately needed as

their mouths began to go dry with nerves.
All the runners who were helping on set
were wishing them good luck, and the
friends discussed tricky bits of their act and
chatted while the clock ticked round to their
appearance time.

Caves 'n' Rocks were on before them and
sang brilliantly. They received a rapturous
response from the audience and the girls felt
sick with stage-fright.

Now it was time to be bold. This was the
moment they had been waiting for; the
moment they thought had been snatched
away from them for ever. They walked out
onto the stage with their arms linked
together. The crowd stood up and cheered,
which was very unexpected but gave the
girls a huge boost of confidence. Then they
all took their positions. Daisy sat at the
drums. Rose walked over to the keyboard.
Lily adjusted her guitar strap and Poppy and

Honey grabbed their tambourines and microphones. They were ready.

Just as Daisy began the intro to the song on the drums, Poppy noticed Lilac standing on her chair right at the front, clapping and screaming wildly. She had kept her promise. Everything felt just right as they launched into their performance.

The girls were note-perfect and Poppy and Honey's dance routine was superb. It passed in a blur of concentration, nerves and fun for Poppy, and when they finished, everyone in the audience stood up and clapped and cheered.

"Again! Again! Encore!" called the audience.

Daisy looked over to the judges, who all nodded. So the girls sang it all over again. Finally they left the stage to a rowdy standing ovation.

The moment when the judges revealed

their decision came quickly. Johnny McDonald stood up, reading from a sheet in front of him. He began the torturous procedure of reading out the results in reverse order.

"In third place, we have little Blossom Darling with *Ballet School Rap*. It was sweet, original and we liked it – you've got real potential, so keep at it. In second place is Caves 'n' Rocks. What  a great boy band, really promising. Keep going, guys! But in first place, the band that will be going to the finals in the City, by unanimous decision of the judges, is . . . the Beach Babes with their brilliant song, *Chocolate Sundae Girls*!"

The crowd's reaction sounded like

thunder. Poppy thought she would faint as
they went back on stage and sang their song
for a final time.

There was a huge fuss after the results,
with cameras flashing and reporters
crowding around. But as she was smiling
and laughing with the rest of the band,
Poppy saw Lilac and her family slip off and
walk away quietly, all looking very sad,
especially Lilac.

"Mum," said Poppy as she was being tucked into bed later that night, exhausted from all the excitement and the celebrations, "why do there have to be winners and losers – it means that the winner is happy and the loser is sad. I don't like other people to feel sad."

"I know what you mean, Poppy. But we all have a mixture of happy times and not so happy times. We should never set out to make other people unhappy though, never, and if you lose something, you should always try to be happy for the winners, just like Lilac was for you in the end. Did you see her clapping and cheering?"

"Yes, Mum," said Poppy, yawning, "but she looked so sad after the competition, and even though what she did was wrong, I don't want her to be sad."

"I'm sure she'll feel better soon, darling. What Lilac did was wrong and it was brave of her to confess, but it is always better to be honest in the first place and then, hopefully, you'll never feel the way Lilac is feeling right now."

Poppy nodded drowsily and reached out to hug her mother. "I just can't wait for all those free chocolate sundaes Fleur promised us!"

Mum giggled. "My little pop star princess," she said, feeling very proud of her eldest daughter, and not just because she had won the contest.

Turn over to read an extract from the next Princess Poppy book,
Ballet Dreams . . .

Chapter One

Poppy always got butterflies in her tummy when her ballet exam was coming up. Her ballet teacher, Madame Angelwing, was always very demanding and ambitious for her girls, but at exam time she really wanted her little ballerinas to perform brilliantly. It was only eight weeks until Lady Margery de Mille, the examiner from the Royal Academy, would come to the Lavender Lake School of Dance to test Poppy and her friends.

One Tuesday, at the end of the weekly ballet class, Madame Angelwing gave all the girls an information sheet about the exam and then talked them through it.

The girls folded the notes into their ballet cases.

"Don't forget to give them to your parents when you get home," said Madame

115

Angelwing, "and, Honey, you give yours to your grandmother. Bye, girls!"

"Goodbye, Madame, see you next week!" they called as they trouped out of the dance school.

Poppy and Honey were both very hungry and thirsty after class so they decided to go to Bumble Bees Teashop for a snack and a drink.

"Hello, girls!" called Granny Bumble as they arrived. "And how was ballet today?"

"Oh, Granny, it was so good," replied Honey breathlessly. "We learned some new steps and Madame Angelwing told us all about the exam. We're going to have to do so much practice for it."

"Well, as long as you don't let it take over your lives – there is more to life than ballet, you know," commented Granny Bumble.

"Yeah, I know, but I really, really love it, and Madame Angelwing says that I could be a proper ballerina one day if I work hard, and I want to get Honours in the exam. Oh, and Granny, another thing," continued Honey, "Madame Angelwing says that we need new ballet outfits for the exam – look, she's given us a list. She says that we have to get everything from Ballet Belles in the City. Can we meet all the ballet girls and their mums this Saturday and go up on the train? Madame said that if we don't go soon, there will be nothing left for us!"

"Well, if everyone else is going, I suppose we'll have to!" agreed Granny, less than cheerfully. "I'll just phone Holly Mallow and see if she can work here on Saturday. Mind you, I don't see what's wrong with the ballet outfits you've all got already."

At the weekend Poppy, Honey, Sweetpea, Mimosa, Abigail, all their mums and Granny Bumble met at the Honeypot Hill Railway Station to go up to the beautiful ballet shop in the city.

"I want a pale pink ballet dress and matching crossover cardigan!" said Sweetpea as they all settled down in their seats.

"I want a pale blue set!" declared Mimosa.

"Wait and see what's available in your size!" said Mimosa's mum.

"Yes, girls, she's right," said Poppy's mum. "You mustn't go setting your heart on things and then being disappointed if you can't have them."

"I'm getting a white leotard with a lilac top," Honey announced.

"Madame Angelwing and her fancy ideas, indeed!" tutted Granny Bumble. "Costs a fortune and you've got plenty of perfectly respectable tutus in the cupboard at home!"

Before long the train arrived at their destination. Everyone clambered out and made their way to the main shopping district.

"Here's Ballet Belles!" called Poppy, recognizing the heavenly ballet shop she had visited a couple of times before with Mum.

Everyone followed her in. They had a lovely time in the ballet shop looking at the rows of shell-pink satin ballet shoes, some with points like the older girls wore, and rails of pastel-coloured ballet dresses. Poppy loved all the other pretty accessories too, such as satin ballet cases with mirrors inside, ballerina jewel boxes, hair bands and ribbons. There were also shelves of books about ballet.

"Look at all these pretty swans!" said

Poppy as she and Honey flicked through a beautifully illustrated book about *Swan Lake*. "One day that will be you, Honey," she said proudly, pointing to a picture of a ballerina floating through the air.

Honey smiled. She absolutely adored ballet and she really hoped that one day she *would* be a ballerina, just like Madame Angelwing had been.

An hour or so later, after much choosing and trying on of outfits, everyone eventually found something that was just perfect, so they made their purchases and decided to go to an outdoor café in the old flower market area. The girls feasted on chocolate-chip muffins and frothy strawberry milkshakes and the grown-ups had creamy lattes and chocolate shortcake. At tea time they made their way back to the railway station and boarded the homeward train, feeling tired after their exciting ballet day.